PAUL MORTON

BUG BELLY
FROGGY RESCUE

FIVE QUILLS

RAVEN
ROCKS

MAGPIE NEST

OLD CHESTNUT TREE

BUG BELLY

FROGGY
RESCUE

For my brother Dean, Katja, Gian and Nina.

Can you find a silver key in this book?

BUG BELLY: FROGGY RESCUE
First published in Great Britain in 2021 by Five Quills
93 Oakwood Court, London W14 8JZ

www.fivequills.co.uk

Five Quills and associated logos are a trademark of Five Quills Ltd.

Text and illustrations copyright © Paul Morton 2021

The right of Paul Morton to be identified as the author
and illustrator of this work has been asserted.

Edited by Natascha Biebow at Blue Elephant Storyshaping
Designed by Amy Cooper

A CIP record for this title is available from the British Library

ISBN 978 1 912923 05 2

1 3 5 7 9 10 8 6 4 2

Printed in Croatia by INK69

TOP POND

MIDDLE POND

BOTTOM POND

WHISPERING WOODS

THE WATERSIDE
18 HOLE GOLF COURSE

BUG BELLY AND FROGLETS

BUG BELLY

Bug Belly is famous for his ingenious plans, clever kit bag and cool gadgets. He's **ALWAYS** hungry!

SPLASH

The one in the middle. She is a do-gooder with a heart of gold.

SPLISH

Splish is the most grown-up of all the froglets. Bug Belly can trust him to take charge.

SPLODGE

Splodge is the youngest. He's always getting into trouble.

OWL

NAME: Swoopus silentii
EATS: Anything small
LIVES: Whispering Woods
FRIENDS: Other owls
ENEMIES: Large hawks

MAGPIE

NAME: Theavus thug
EATS: Most small creatures
LIVES: Old Chestnut Tree
FRIENDS: Not many
ENEMIES: Large owls and foxes

SNEAKY SNAKE

NAME: Slytherus Sneakus
EATS: Tadpoles and froglets
LIVES: Wherever food goes
FRIENDS: Other snakes
ENEMIES: Owls and hawks

Chapter 1

"**Whooooaaaahh!** just look at THOSE sparkles!" cried Bug Belly.

He grinned at the three froglets lying next to him on the lily leaf. Splish, Splash and Splodge were enjoying a sleepover with their favourite uncle in Bottom Pond.

"Fireworks?" asked Splodge, staring in wonder at the starry night sky.

"**Noooo.** Shooting stars. And shooting stars are **LUCKY,**" Bug Belly said.

"Let's all make a wish before bedtime."

"Ooh me first," Splish said. "I wish . . . I could go on mega-exciting adventures."

"And I wish . . . um . . . I wish I wasn't so scared of water!" Splash blushed.

"Fancy a frog that can't swim!" sang Splodge.

He thought for a moment, then shouted, "I wish I could **FLY!**"

"Frogs can't **FLY**," snapped Splash. "And I can't help it if I'm not a good swimmer!"

"I wish I could **fly** on my own shooting star," said Splodge.

Bug Belly munched on some spider snacks. "Wow, great wishes!"

"What about you, Uncle Bug Belly?"

"Mmmmm, that's easy. I'd like a never-ending buffet of delumptious bugs."

He patted his gurgling tum and fell asleep dreaming about a big breakfast bug hunt.

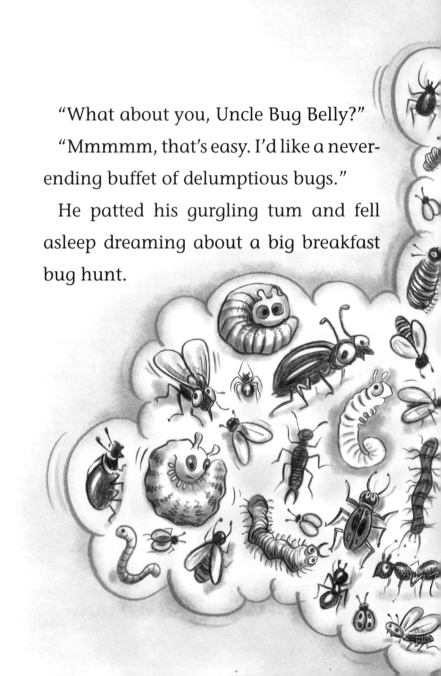

Chapter 2

Early the next morning Bug Belly was busy gobbling up grasshoppers when, without warning . . .

SPLOOOOOOOSH!!

Something blazed brightly overhead and blasted into the pond.

"Fizzing frogspawn! Was that a shooting star from last night?" Bug Belly spluttered.

It glimmered and shimmered at the bottom of the pond.

Splish dived to fetch it. "It looks like a meteorite from Mars."

"No," whispered Splodge, grabbing it. "Don't you see? It's my wish coming true! It's my shooting star!"

Splash knew a thing or two about astronomy and explained, "Actually, a meteorite **IS** a shooting star, but it's highly unlikely one would plop into our pond, especially in the daytime!"

"Well, I think it **IS** a star," said Splodge, "and I'm going to keep it. **Can** I keep it, Uncle Bug Belly?"

But Bug Belly wasn't listening. His tummy had just gone

URGLE-GURGLE GLUMP!

All he could think about was breakfast.

At that very moment a distant dot in the sky changed direction and darted towards the pond. Bug Belly would have spotted the danger straightaway. He knew about these things.

But unfortunately his head was stuck in a snail shell . . .

Chapter 3

When Bug Belly **DID** see the approaching danger, he coughed on a mouthful of snail and spluttered, "Great galloping grasshoppers, drop the star, Splodge, drop it **NOW!**"

Splash screamed. Splish pointed.

But the youngest froglet had his back to the danger. In a black and white feathery flash, Splodge **AND** his star disappeared.

"What on earth?" said Splash.

Bug Belly pointed to the large bird, carrying Splodge off into the sky. "Thieving magpies. They steal anything bright and shiny. That one must've spotted the star and snatched poor Splodge at the same time."

This was a disaster!

"Wh-where has he gone?" whimpered Splish.

"To the magpie's nest," scowled Bug Belly.

"Will we ever see him again?" Splash's bottom lip trembled. "Splodge wanted to fly, but not like that! We've **GOT** to rescue him!"

"We **WILL** get him back, I promise," said Bug Belly. "But it won't be easy. Those rotten magpies nest in the Old Chestnut Tree, on the river bend at the far edge of Whispering Woods."

"Whispering Woods?" gulped Splash. "B-but . . . they're dangerous."

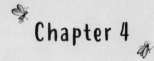

Chapter 4

Bug Belly nodded. "Yes, but the fastest way to rescue Splodge is straight **THROUGH** the woods. So that means . . . we're going to need one of my super-duper plans."

Bug Belly opened his kit bag and got to work right away. He chomped on a caterpillar chew to help him concentrate. He made measurements, scribbled notes, doodled diagrams and drew up a list. Then in a burst of Bug Belly brilliance, he came up with his . . .

most brilliant ever rescue plan.

"It's going to be tricky, it's going to be tight, but **THIS** is what we'll do," he told the froglets.

MOST BRILLIANT EVER RESCUE PLAN
part 1

TOP POND →

MIDDLE POND

BOTTOM POND →

MAGPIE NEST

WHISPERING WOODS
(DANGER!)

OLD CHESTNUT
TREE

. . . .
Quickest way to the nest!

"The journey will be dangerous, so we'll need these."

Backpacks with surprise fold-out flaps.

Bug Belly handed Splish and Splash a backpack each.

Scary view from the back!

"Pop them on and lift out the special flaps, like this, see?"

"RAAAAAH!"

Splash flapped her arms and howled. "Look! We're two fierce monsters. If Sneaky Snake comes creeping now she's in for a shock."

Splish laughed, then said sadly, "But we should be **three** monsters. Splodge would have loved these."

"Yes you're right, he would," sighed Bug Belly. "Come on! We need to rescue Splodge before he becomes a magpie mini-meal." Bug Belly quickly led the way out of Bottom Pond, over the river and into . . .

. . . **Whispering Woods**.

Chapter 5

The three frogs picked their way nervously through the creepy woods, hurrying towards the Old Chestnut Tree. The branches creaked in the wind, and suddenly, they heard . . .

URGLE-GURGLE
GLUMP!

"Oh no! There goes my hungry tum alarm." Bug Belly frowned. "Hmm, **IS** there time for a quick bug hunt?" He thought for a moment. "Oh, go on then, quickly, to keep our strength up."

Splish cheered and soon wrestled a wiggly wriggler into his mouth.

"Nice," said Bug Belly, busily slurping down a slug. Then he grabbed three juicy grubs. But instead of eating them, he mysteriously slipped them into his kit bag. "For later." He winked. "Come on, let's keep going."

The three frogs walked and hopped and walked all day until Bug Belly spotted a bat. "It'll be dark soon. Time to camp for the night," he announced.

"My legs **ARE** dropping off," wailed Splish wearily. "But they only need a **SHORT** rest."

Hoohooooot!

"Oh, don't let me be Owl's froggy fritter snack!" Splash whimpered. She shuffled closer to her uncle.

"Not on my watch!" Uncle Bug Belly reassured her.

Bug Belly reached into his kit bag and took out the grubs. He plopped them into jars. "Ooh delicious," said Splish.

"No, wait!" cried Bug Belly. "Don't eat them. Just shake and . . .

Splish and Splash's faces lit up.

"Glow worms," said Bug Belly. "Cool, huh?" He handed the froglets some scrummy marsh midges to toast for supper. They munched, happily hunched over the warm, glowing jars.

Then Splish swallowed slowly as though he had a lump in his throat. "I wish Splodge were here."

"Don't worry," said his uncle, "we'll reach the magpie nest early tomorrow."

Splash yawned.

"Bedtime," said Bug Belly. "Slip off your backpacks and we'll light them up to keep guard . . . That should scare off owls, snakes and other night-time prowlers!" He chuckled.

They soon fell fast asleep and so never noticed two eyes watching hungrily from the shadows.

If they had known then
that the three frogs would
become only two,
they wouldn't have
slept a wink!

Chapter 6

The next morning a thick fog surrounded everything.

"Blistering bumblebees! How will we ever find the Old Chestnut Tree in this?" Bug Belly said.

They'd only just set off when Bug Belly froze. Splash banged into his bottom.

"Sorry, I couldn't see in the fog."

"The fog isn't our only trouble. Listen!"

Splash heard it. Something nearby was hissing.

Hisssssssssss

"Oh no, that's not . . . is it . . .?" whispered Splash.

"Flaming fire ants!" said Bug Belly. "It's Sneaky Snake. She must have been following us all along."

"I'm going to end up a lump in a snake's tum!" cried Splash.

"Not if I can help it. Quick, off with your backpack," ordered Bug Belly. "Stuff it with this stinky rabbit poo and stand it on that stump."

In the fog, it looked just like a juicy fat frog.

"A yucky, mucky surprise for an unlucky snake!" sneered Bug Belly.

Blergh!

"Now, quick, let's skedaddle. Where's Splish?"

"Isn't he with you?" asked Splash, panic-stricken.

"Walloping wasps!" wailed Bug Belly. "Splodge taken, and now **Splish has disappeared!**"

"Whatever will I tell your mums and dads?!" Bug Belly took a deep breath. "OK, he can't have gone far. Listen. That must be the river so we're probably getting close to the Old Chestnut Tree." He took one step forward and stopped again. "Quickly, there's something else following us now, look!"

A single blue glowing 'eye' stumbled through the fog towards them.

"We're going to be gobbled up by a one-eyed river monster!" Splash cried out.

"Shhh, squeeze in behind these rocks,"
said Bug Belly.
The monster wobbled closer.
The monster whimpered.

SNIFFLE!

WIMPER!

SOB!

"Hang on a minute," said Bug Belly. "Monsters don't whimper."

"They do if they're hungry baby monsters who've lost their monster mum," moaned Splash. Then, just at the very worst possible moment, Bug Belly's tummy gave a loud . . .

URGLE-GURGLE GLUMP!

Chapter 7

The monster heard it. It dashed towards them . . .

"Uncle B–Bug Belly???!"

"Who?! What?" stuttered Bug Belly. "Spitting spiders, it's Splish!"

Splish sprung forward, his face weirdly illuminated by a blue glow from his belly. "Oh, thank goodness, I've found you. I g-g-got lost in the fog. Then I got hungry. And I swallowed that glow-bug-thingy so now my tummy's lit up like a lightbulb. And look . . .

". . . I've even got glow-in-the-dark poo!"

After a few seconds of shocked silence, they all collapsed in fits of laughter. Splash told Splish about the near miss with Sneaky Snake. They laughed all over again.

Then Bug Belly said, "Quickly, now, we **HAVE** to find that Old Chestnut Tree and rescue Splodge!"

OoooooOOofff!

Bug Belly let out a painful cry as his nose bumped into something hard. "Fizzing fireflies!

I think I've found it!"

The three frogs looked up and up, **AND UP**, to the magpie's nest at the top of the tree.

"Whooooah!"

"No way. We can't reach that! It's impossible," gasped Splish.

Chapter 8

"Sounds like it's time for part 2 of my plan!" said Bug Belly.

The froglets' jaws dropped in disbelief at their uncle's preposterous plan.

"Bats fly, magpies fly, but frogs **CAN'T** fly!" said Splish.

"**OH, YES, THEY CAN!**" Bug Belly said with a confident grin. "You'll soon see. That's the best bit! Now, let's get cracking."

MOST BRILLIANT EVER RESCUE PLAN
part 2

FLY TO TOP OF TREE

1. Find a log.

2. Tie a pebble to one end of the string.

3. Load pebble into catapult and . . .

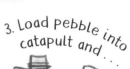

Magpie's nest

Old Chestnut Tree

4. Shoot pebble over branch.

AIM * HERE

SEE NEXT PAGE ▷

"Splish, you collect mud face paint, feathers and some thorny twigs for my disguise. Oh and four nice, fat worms. Ooh, no, make it seven. We'll scoff one each now. Splash, we'll need four of those long leaves please. I'll look for a dry log."

Bug Belly returned puffing, dragging the log into position on the edge of the river bank under the tree.

Then he reached into his kit bag. He tied the end of a ball of string to a pebble. Next, he handed his nephew his catapult.

"Shoot this string, up and over that thick branch, the one above the nest. Quickly now, whilst I get ready."

Splish hesitated, not sure if he could do it. The pebble bounced back so many times that he was getting frantic.

Then

BINGO!...

. . . it soared over the
branch and dropped
back down the other side.

"Brilliant," said Bug Belly. "You tie the pebble end to the log. I'll fasten this end to my kit bag." He tugged on the string. "Perfect."

Next, Bug Belly got started on his disguise to scare the magpie: he smeared on his mud face paint and attached feathers to his arms.

"Now, time to rescue Splodge from right under that thieving Magpie's **cheeky sneaky beak!**"

Splish and Splash looked horrified. "But what if she's in the nest?"

"Then she'll get a **BIG BUG BELLY** surprise! I'll rescue Splodge from the nest, parachute down, and then we'll all escape back home using the river. Any questions?!"

The froglets looked stunned.

"Er, this might sound silly," said Splash. "I know that we're frogs. And frogs are supposed to **LIKE** swimming.

But, that river is so fast, so fierce, I can't possibly swim in **THAT!**"

"You won't have to swim," said Bug Belly.

"Part 3 of my plan is the **BEST BIT!**"

MOST BRILLIANT EVER RESCUE PLAN
part 3

HOME PLAN

Chestnut tree leaf

1. Me and Splodge parachute back down from the nest to the river.

2. Splish and Splash are ready waiting with the long leaves for our speedy getaway!

Use them as surf boards.

3. We all surf back home on the fast river.

Bug Belly held up the long leaves that Splash had collected. "We'll **RIVER SURF** back home on these. When I drop back down with Splodge, have them ready. We'll need to make a very speedy getaway."

Then he roared,

RAAAAAAAH!

"How do I look?"

"Magnificently menacing!" Splash and Splash shouted.

"Excellent! Now, roll that log!"

Chapter 9

The froglets heaved the log down the river bank. It bounced into the whooshing water, pulling the string behind it. The string ran up and over the branch and down to Bug Belly's kit bag. When the log bobbed back to the surface of the river, it was swept away in the choppy current. This made the string go tight. With a **TWANG!** Bug Belly launched skywards.

He rocketed up into the tree, past startled spiders and baffled beetles. Bug Belly's tum rumbled at the sight of all those tasty treats . . . But then he remembered Splodge.

He looked around, scanning for danger. "Bumbling beetles!" Bug Belly exclaimed in horror. Magpie was home. She was sitting **IN THE NEST!**

Bug Belly landed on the branch above Magpie and cut himself loose. Fanning out his fearsome feathers, he took a deep breath. Then, with a terrifying battle croak he launched himself at the nest.

"SHOWTIME!"

The surprised bird gawped at the weird bat – or was it a ferocious hawk? – dropping straight towards her. Squawking in shock, Magpie scrambled from the tree and flapped away.

Bug Belly laughed as he landed on the nest, ditching his costume. But his smile soon faded.

There was no sign of Splodge anywhere!

Chapter 10

Bug Belly crept towards the centre of the nest. He tripped over shiny magpie treasures and squeezed past a cracked egg. Suddenly, something turned and stared straight at him.

A magpie chick!

Bug Belly's heart thumped. "Oh, boiled beetlejuice, don't be thinking I'm **YOUR** all-day breakfast, ugly mugly! Here, have these instead."

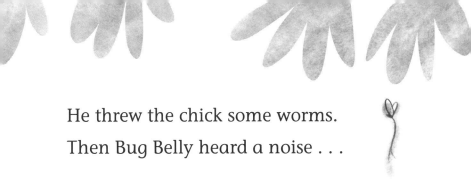

He threw the chick some worms.

Then Bug Belly heard a noise . . .

He whipped round and watched horrified as the top of the egg wobbled off. A soggy, froggy head popped out, dripping in bird droppings and yucky egg gunk.

"Uncle Bug Belly? Is it **REALLY** you?" Splodge fell sobbing out of his hiding place and gave his uncle a big squelchy bird-pooey hug. Bug Belly squeezed him back.

"Oh, I was scared the chick would eat me. But it's not eating solids yet, well, at least not solid frogs, and—!"

"Shhh, Splodge!" Bug Belly interrupted. "We've got to go. Magpie will be back **ANY SECOND**."

Bug Belly tore off a couple of large leaves and thrust one into Splodge's hand. "Use this to parachute down. Splish and Splash are waiting. Ready?"

"1, 2, 3 JUMP!"

Bug Belly leapt
off the branch.

"WAIT!" shouted
Splodge. "My STAR!"
He dashed back into the nest to fetch it . . .

Chapter 11

Bug Belly was already half-way down when he realised that Splodge hadn't jumped. In the distance he spotted not one magpie, but **TWO** coming towards them.

"Splodge, **WHERE ARE YOU?**" he cried.

Splodge stood, clutching his star, on the edge of the branch. He wanted to fly, but . . . "Whoooa, I didn't know we were **THIS** high up," he wailed. His legs turned to jelly and it felt like a fish was doing a flippy-flop in his tummy.

Bug Belly looked up and yelled, **"SPLODGE, JUMP!** The magpies are coming!"

It worked. Bug Belly saw Splodge's legs buckle. The shooting star slipped. Splodge caught it between his knees, toppled forwards and fell, holding tightly to the leaf.

He grinned from ear to ear, thrilled to be flying on his very own shooting star.

From mid-fall, Bug Belly could see three things:

1. above, Splodge flying towards him
2. in the distance, **TWO** magpies speeding towards them
3. below, Splish and Splash, ready with the getaway leaves.

But also . . . Horrifyingly, behind Splish and Splash, was the slinky, slithering shape of Sneaky Snake!

Bug Belly's eyes bulged with terror.

"Oh no, not Sneaky Snake, not now! **LOOK OUT!**" he cried. But Splish and Splash couldn't hear him from so far away.

They simply smiled and waved back at their uncle.

Bug Belly needed to think quickly.

He looked up at Splodge sailing down on his shooting star.

This gave him a wild idea. "It's our only chance!" he decided out loud. "Splodge," he shouted, "you **MUST** let go of the star, **EXACTLY** when I tell you."

Then the magpies attacked.

Jamming his leaf parachute into his mouth, Bug Belly fished out a puffball from his kit bag. He banged his hands together like popping a paper bag.

A thick cloud of mushroom dust exploded into the magpies' faces, stinging their eyes. Coughing and spluttering, the choking birds crashed headfirst into each other, then flapped off.

Below, the waiting froglets had no idea that right behind them, Sneaky Snake was about to strike, her mouth stretched wide.

Bug Belly gulped.

"**NOW**, Splodge, **NOW!** Drop the star **NOW!**" Bug Belly bellowed.

Splodge wasn't sure what was happening. He really didn't want to lose his star, but he could tell that Uncle Bug Belly was absolutely deadly serious. So, reluctantly, he dropped it.

Chapter 12

The star hurtled straight into the gaping mouth of the gobsmacked snake. Her jaws snapped shut. Her eyes popped out.

This wasn't the froggy snack she'd expected!

Glaaarrrrh!

"What's up, Sneaky, **NOT** got a frog in your throat?!" laughed Bug Belly.

Seconds later, he and Splodge crash-landed, rolling onto the leafy forest floor. Splish and Splash ran to hug them.

"Hugs later!" shouted Bug Belly. "Go, go, **GO**, before anything else fancies froggy nibbles. **INTO THE RIVER. NOW!**"

Shrieking and whooping, the four frogs rode the rushing river all the way back to the safety of Bottom Pond.

Splash suddenly realised she was no longer afraid of the water. "I'm such a coooool surf dude now!" She beamed.

"And I'm **SO** definitely a **REAL** adventurer," Splish said.

"I really DID fly on my own shooting star," Splodge grinned.

"I'll tell you two things that we all learned!" their uncle said.

"1. Sneaky Snakes **REALLY** don't like **GOBSTOPPERS!** . . . and . . . 2. **ALWAYS BURY YOUR POO IF IT GLOWS IN THE DARK!!!!**"

When they'd finished laughing, he added, "Adventures ALWAYS make me humungously hungry. So, before your mums and dads get back, let's make MY wish come true too and grab some grubalicious bugs! That definitely **IS** the best part of my plan!"

And as Bug Belly smacked his lips, his tummy went . . .

BUG BELLY IS BABYSITTING THE TADPOLES WHEN
TOP POND BEGINS TO EMPTY. CAN HE SAVE THEM
ALL FROM GETTING STUCK IN THE MUD?!

Also available as an E-Book
from online retailers.

www.fivequills.co.uk